The Brilliant Bassoon Book of

Easy Tunes

from

Around the World

for

Bassoon

70 Traditional melodies and rounds from 30 countries arranged especially for beginner Bassoonplayers starting with the very easiest and progressing.

Most are without vent key notes

Amanda Oosthuizen

The Brilliant Bassoon Series

We hope you enjoy *Easy Tunes from Around the World*.
Further copies are available from: http://amazon.com

In case of difficulty, please contact the author direct:

theflyingflute@live.co.uk

Take a look at other exciting books in the series,
including *50 Greatest Classics for Bassoon*,
Catch the Beat, Dazzling Diamonds and *Little Gems for Flute*.
For more information on other intriguing books please go to:
http://theflyingflute.com

© Copyright 2013 Amanda Oosthuizen

The music in this book is protected by copyright and may not be reproduced in any way for sale or private use without the consent of the author.

Contents

A Canoa Virou 9
Ah Ya Zein 25
A My Roschist Chistili... 8
Aura Lee 5
Boat on Lake.. 4
Botany Bay 21
Cader Idris.. 34
Can Can.. 21
Clown's Dance... 7
Come and Sing Together... 26
Dame Tartine 13
David of the White Rock... 35
Don't Forget Katie 32
Early One Morning 28
Everybody Loves Saturday Night 29
French Round 13
Giants 3
Greensleeves 36
Go Down Moses... 24
Hey Ho Nobody At Home.. 26
Hine e Hine 4
House of the Rising Sun.. 33
I Gave My Love a Cherry 31
I Love Sixpence 27
In Spain 15
Izika Zumba 20
Jiana 22
J'ai un Bon Tabac... 15
Johnny Todd 30
Kaake Kaake Koodevide 16
Kisnay Baniya 23
Kookaburra 10
La Bergamesca... 9
La Folia 23
Lightly Row 14
Lullaby (Basque) 24
Lullaby (Polish) 13
Matilda 10
Miss Lucy Long.. 37
Morning Has Broken 17
My Bird is Dead 27
My Dame Hath a Lame Tame Crane 19
Nini ya Moumou 15

Song	Page
Old MacDonald…	6
Obwisana	6
Phoebe in her Petticoat…	9
Pokare Kare	7
Rose Rose	28
Scarborough Fair	31
Seal Woman's Lament	18
Shenandoah	33
Skip to my Lou	17
Sleep Sleep	2
Soley	15
Spanish Ladies	19
The Cuckoo	20
The Dove	5
The Harp that Once Through Tara's Halls	16
This Land is My Land	3
The Londonderry Air	38
This Old Man	30
The Old Tree	2
The Saints	14
The Snow Fell Gently	18
The Three Friends	11
The Three Ravens	25
Tsetang Choung-La	22
Twinkle Twinkle	29
When I First Came to This Land	11
Whisky Johnny	11
Yangtse Boatman	8
Yankee Doodle	2

Information

Tempo Markings
Adagio – slow and stately
Adagio lamentoso – slowly and sadly
Alla Marcia – like a march
Allegretto – moderately fast
Allegretto pomposo – fast and pompous
Allegro – fast and bright
Allegro assai – very fast
Allegro grazioso – fast and gracefully
Allegro maestoso – fast and majestically
Allegro vivace – fast and lively
Andante – at walking speed
Andante maestoso – a majestic walk
Andante moderato – a moderately fast
Andante non troppo – Not too fast
Andantino – slightly faster (or sometimes slower) than Andante
Andantino ingueno – not fast but with innocence
Lento - slowly
Maestoso - majestically
Moderato - moderately
Moderato con moto – moderately with movement
Molto allegro – very fast
Molto maestoso – very majestically
Presto – extremely fast
Tempo di mazurka – In the time of a mazurka - lively
Tempo di valse – In the time of a waltz
Vivace – lively and fast
Vivo - lively

Tempo Changes
rall. – rallentando – gradually slowing down
rit. – ritenuto – slightly slower

 fermata – pause on this note

Dynamic Markings
dim. – diminuendo – gradually softer
cresc. – crescendo – gradually louder
cresc. poco a poco al fine – gradually louder towards the end

pp – *pianissiomo* – very softly
p – *piano* – softly
mp – *mezzo piano* – moderately soft
mf – *mezzo forte* – moderately loud
f – *forte* – loud
ff – *fortissimo* – very loud

gradually louder

gradually softer

Repeats
D.C. al Coda – return to the beginning and follow signs to Coda ⊕
D.C. al Fine – return to the beginning and play to *Fine*

 A repeated passage is to be played with a different ending.

Articulation
staccato – short and detached
sempre staccato – play staccato throughout

accent – played with attack

tenuto – held – pressured accent

marcato – forcefully

Ornaments
trill – rapid movement to the note above and back or from the note above in Mozart and earlier music.

mordent – three rapid notes – the principal note, the note above and the principal.

acciaccatura – a very quick note

appoggiatura – divide the main note equally between the two notes.

Sleep, Sleep

Dreamily — France

The Old Tree

Very slowly — Germany

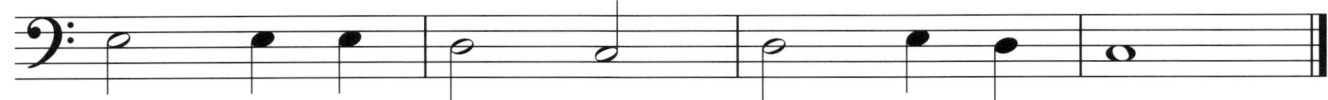

Yankee Doddle

Lively — England

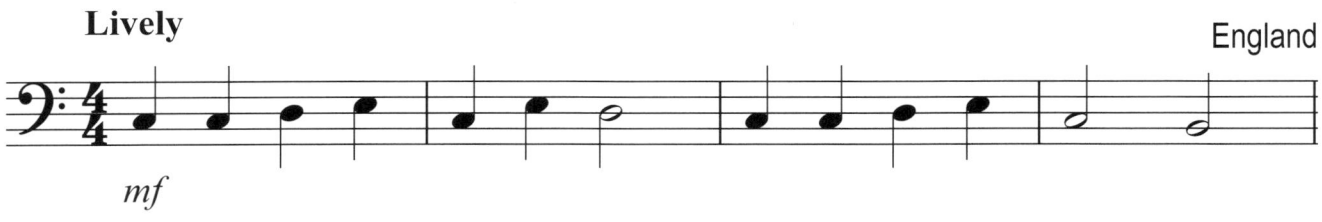

mf

This Land is my Land

Not too fast

USA

Giants

Heavily

Sweden

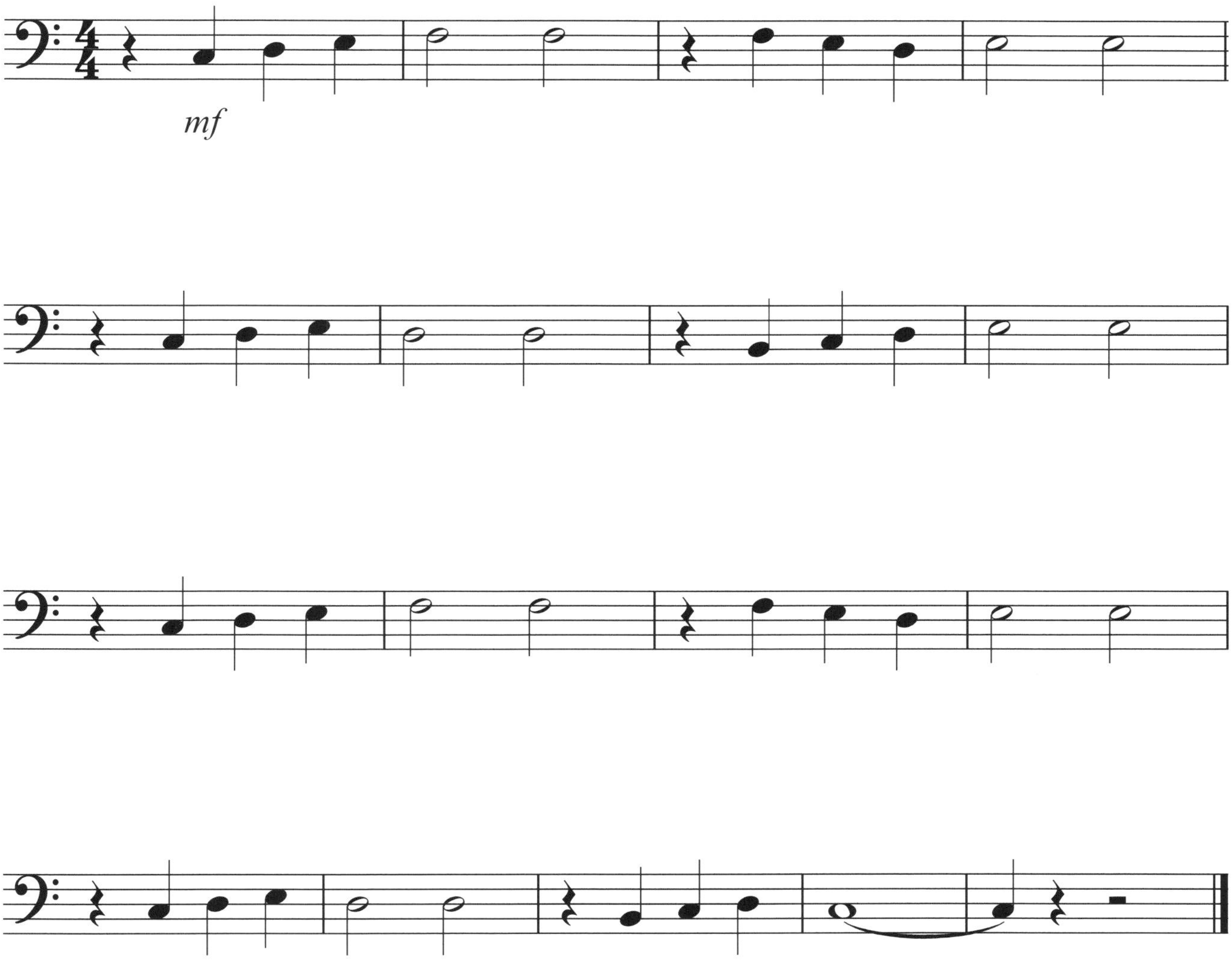

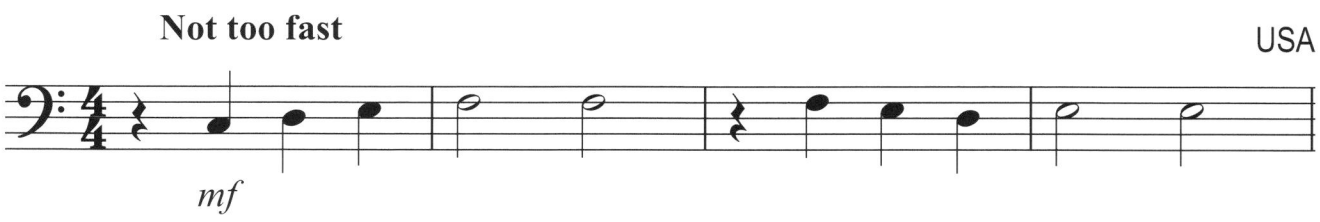

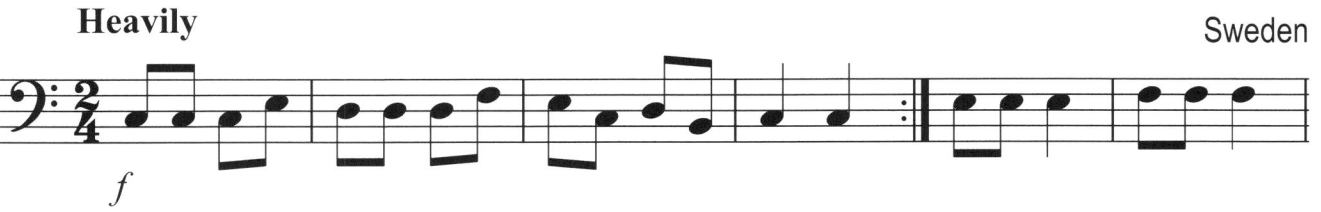

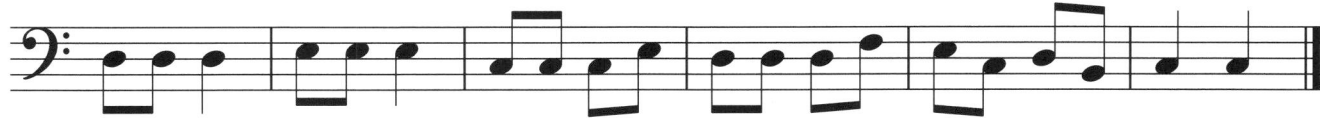

Boat on Lake

Smoothly China

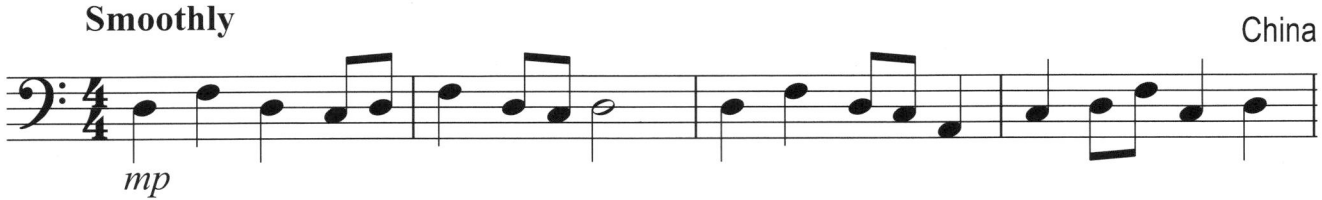

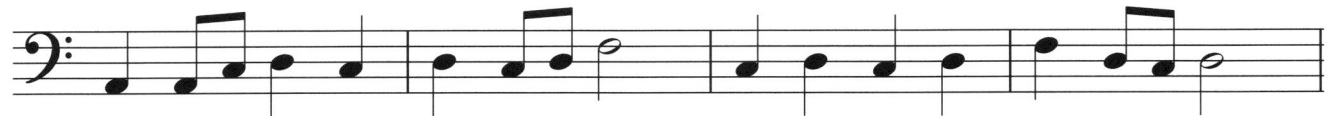

Hine e Hine
(Little Girl)

Sleepily New Zealand

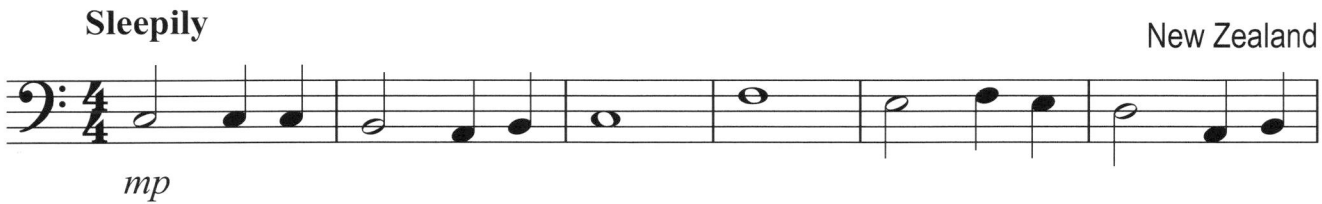

The Dove

Gliding — Wales

Aura Lee

Not too fast — USA

Obwisana
(The rock has hit my hand, Grandma)

Ghana

Fiercely

f

Old MacDonald

Traditional

Lively

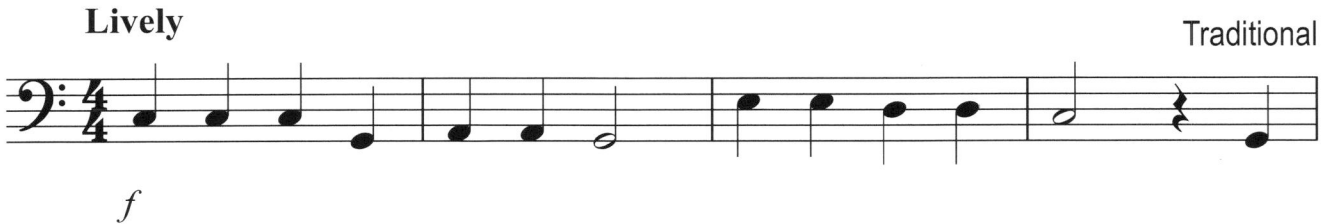

f

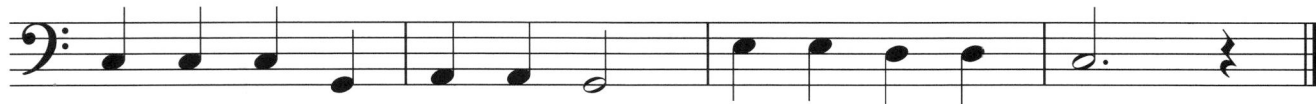

Yangtse Boatman
(a round)

China

As if rowing

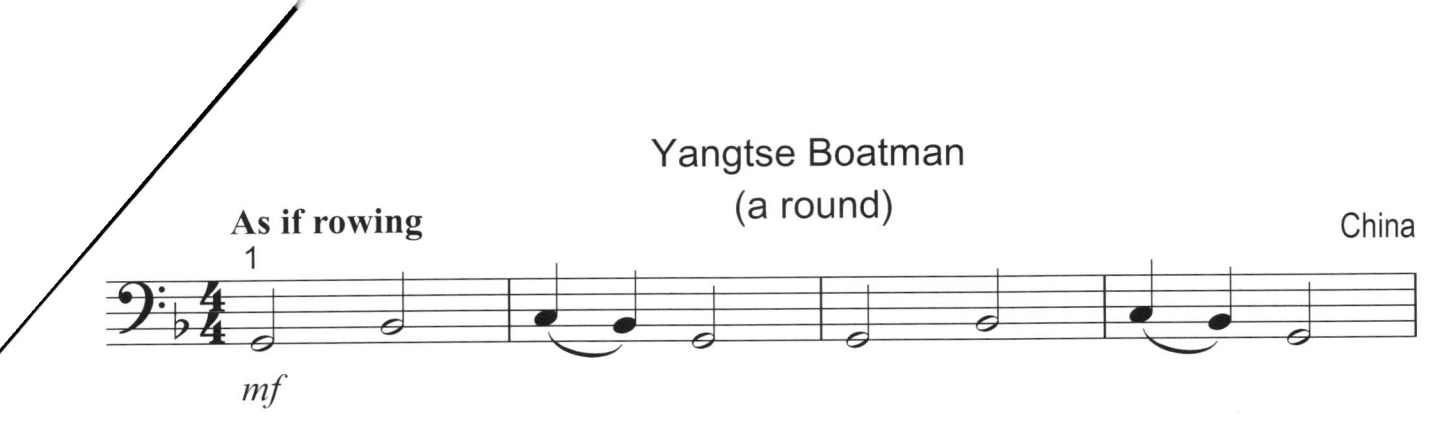

mf

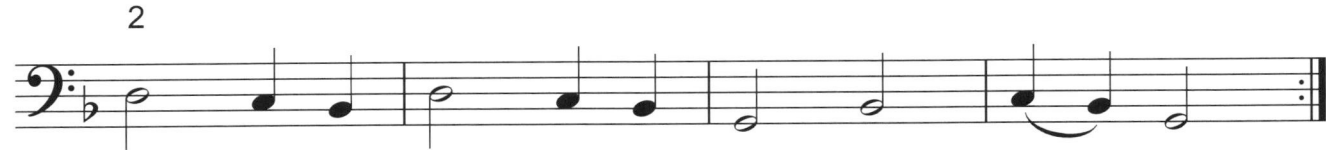

A My Roschist Chistili

Russia

Thoughtfully

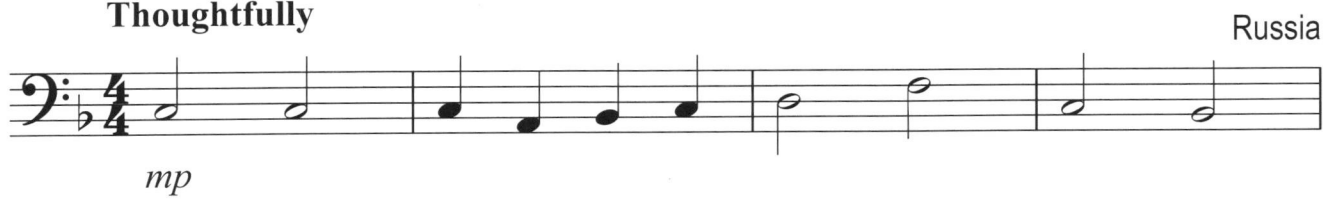

mp

A Canoa Virou
(The Canoe Turned Over)

Running　　　　　　　　　　　　　　　　　　　　　　　　　Brazil

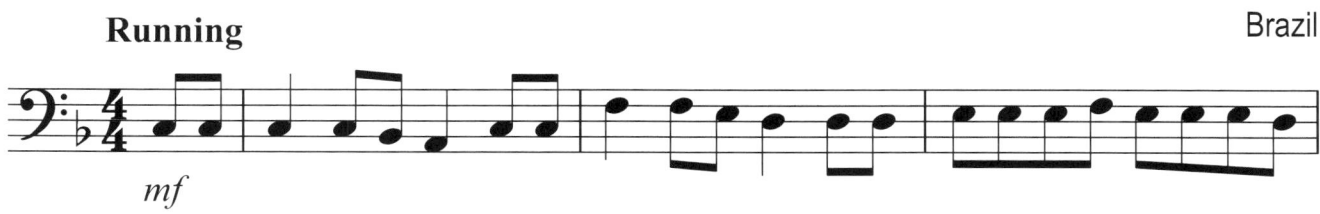

La Bergamesca

Fast　　　　　　　　　　　　　　　　　　　　　　　　　　Italy

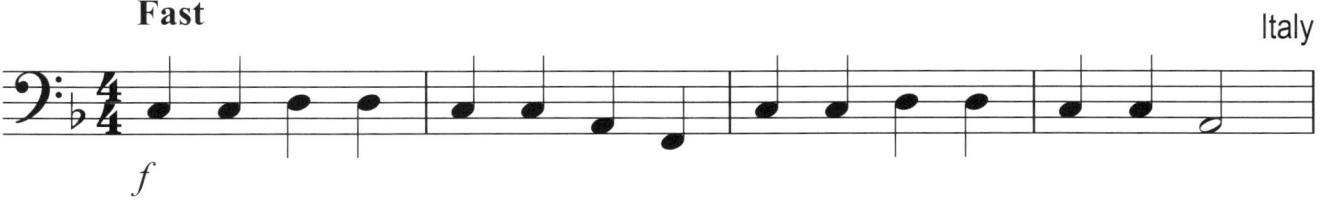

Kookaburra
(a round)

Lively

Australia

Matilda

Lively

Jamaica

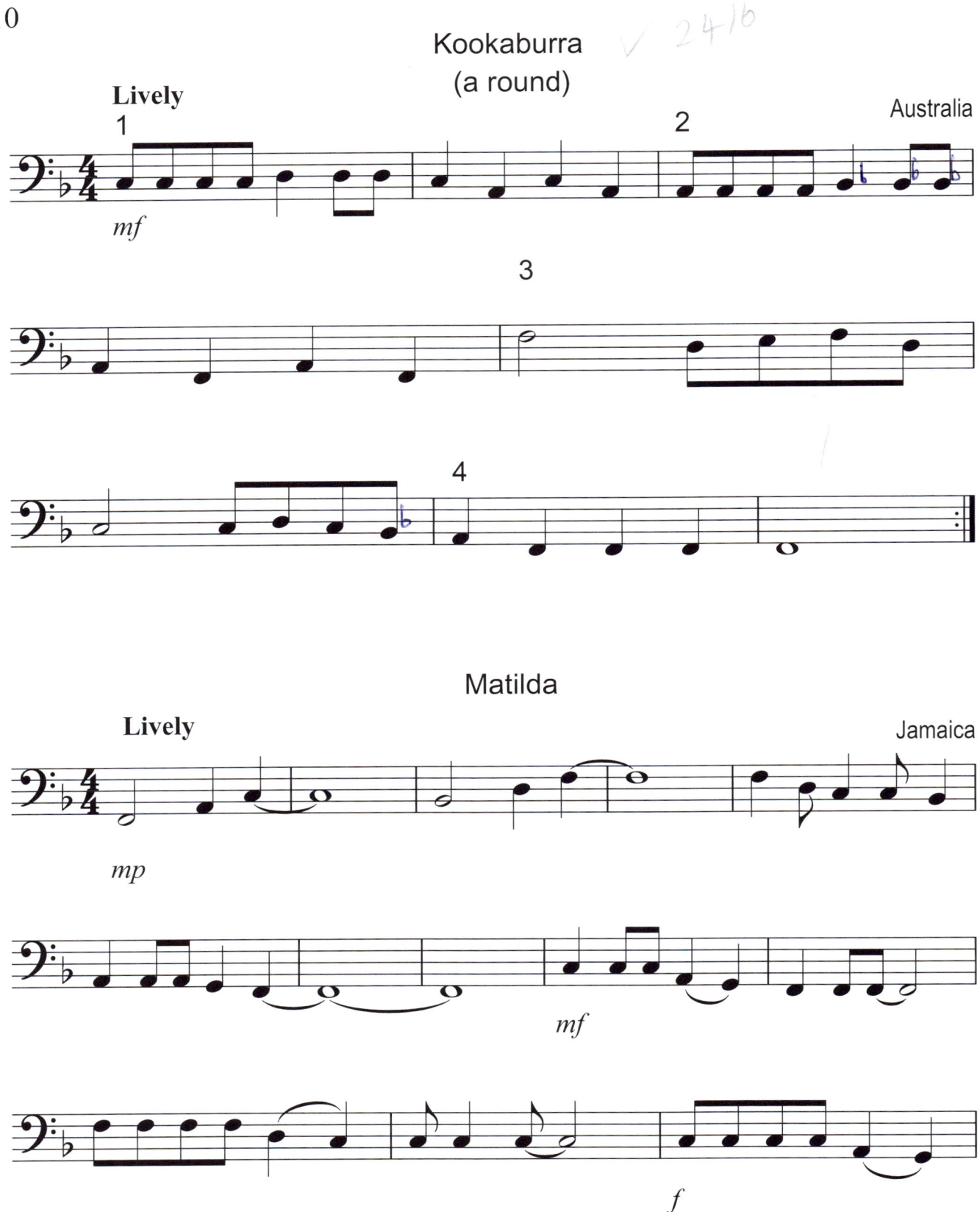

When I First Came to This Land

USA

Phoebe in her Petticoat

England

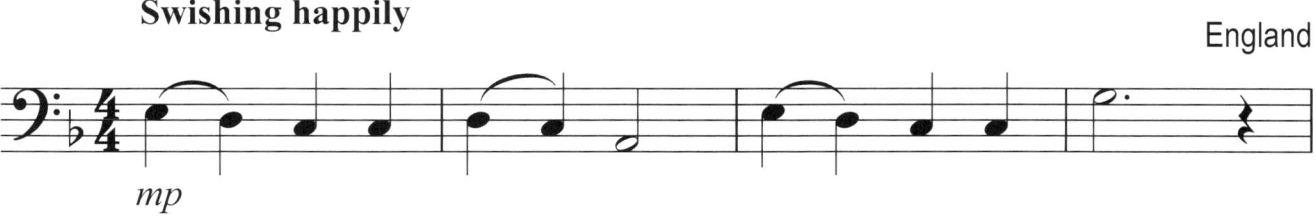

Lullaby

Gently — Poland

French Round

Walking — France

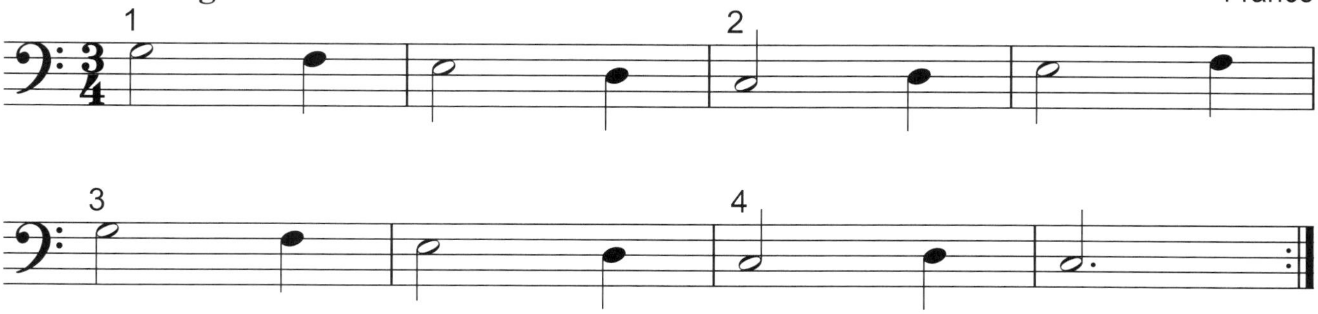

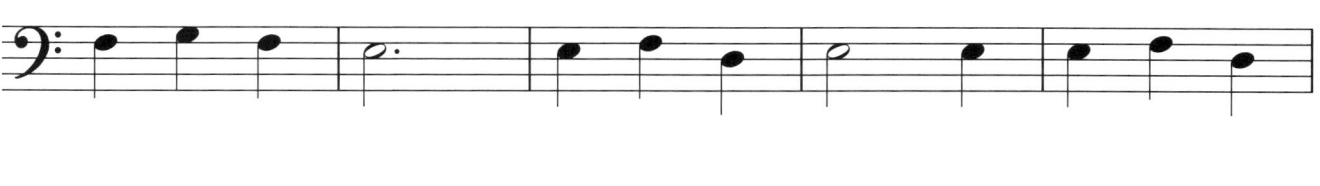

Dame Tartine

Carefully — France

J'ai un Bon Tabac

Lively — France

Fine

D.C. al Fine
(Go to the beginning and play to Fine.)

Nini Ya Moumou
(Sleep, my Baby)

Rocking — Morocco

Soley

Lively — Haiti

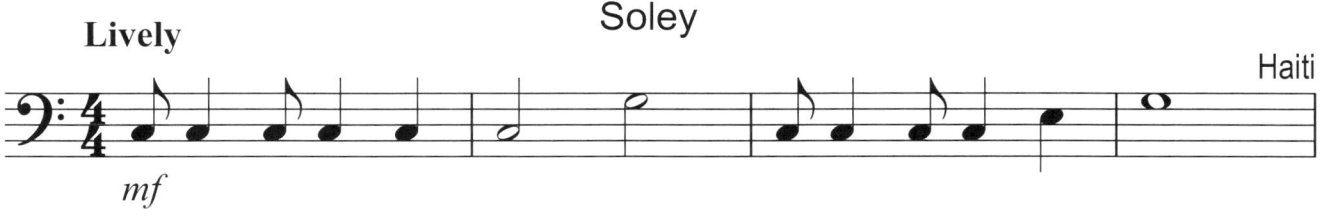

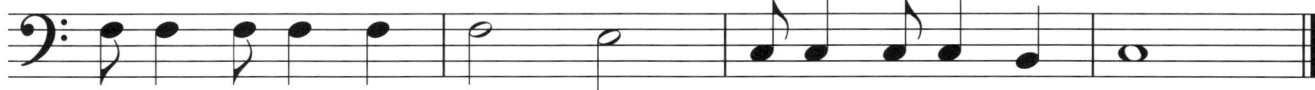

Kakke Kakke Koodevide

(Hey Crow, Where's Your Nest?)

Lively India

The Harp that Once Through Tara's Halls

Not fast Ireland

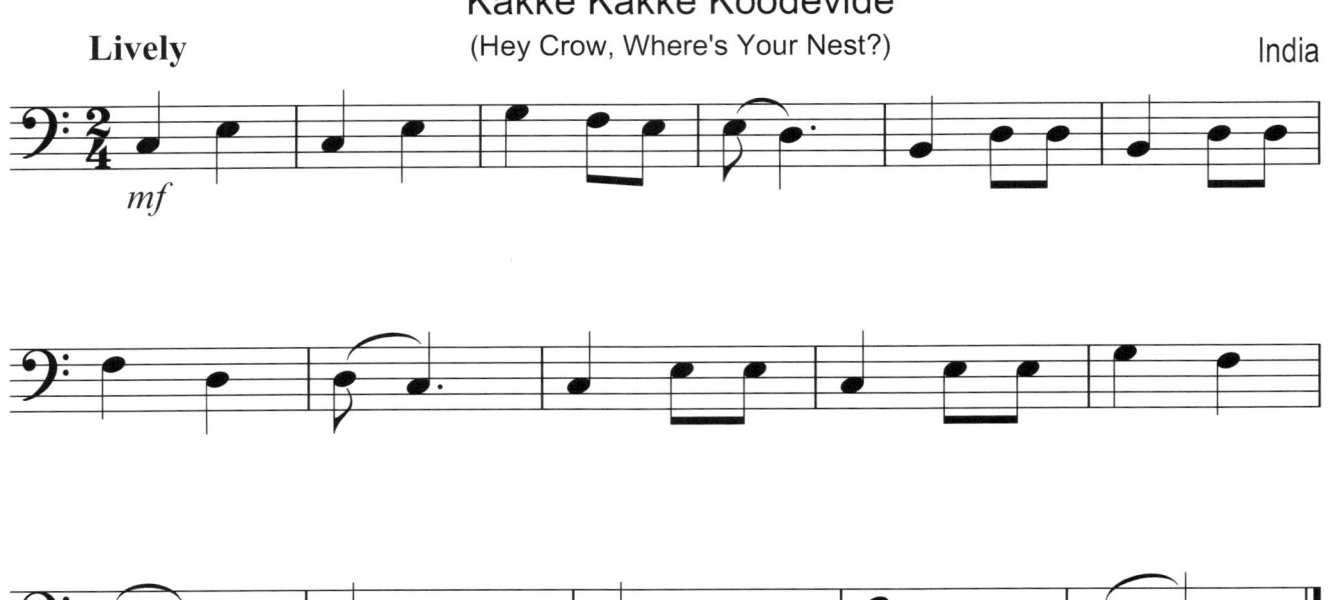

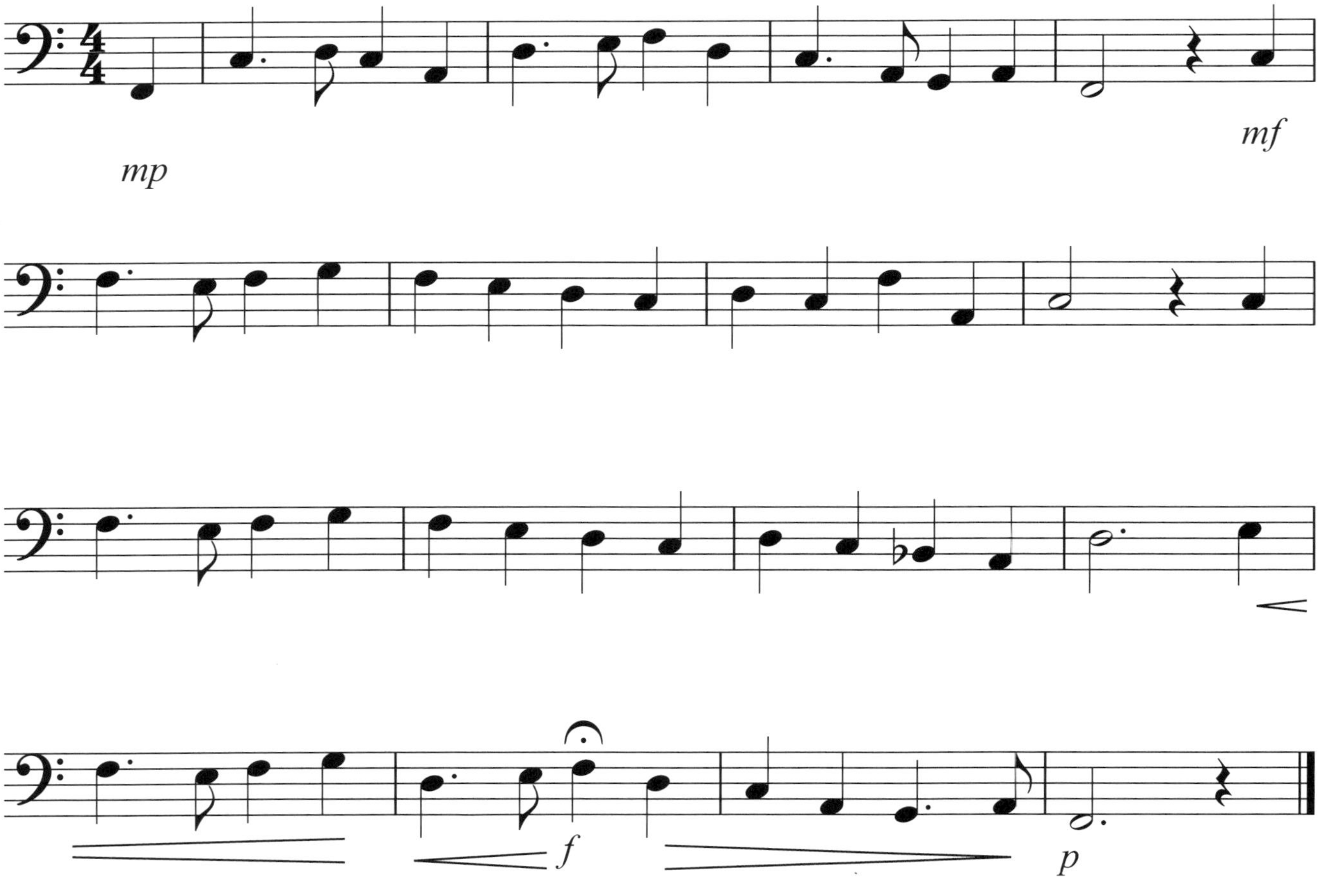

Seal Woman's Lament
(a round)

Iceland

The Snow Fell Softly

Lithuania

My Dame Hath a Lame Tame Crane
(a round)

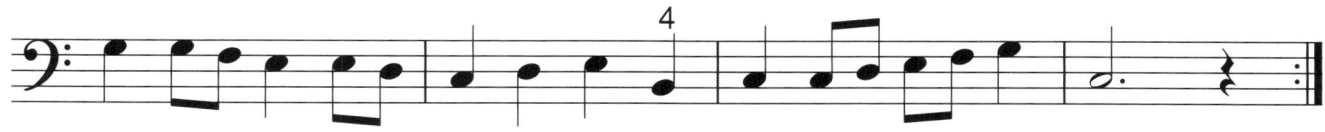

Spanish Ladies

The Cuckoo

Cheerfully — France

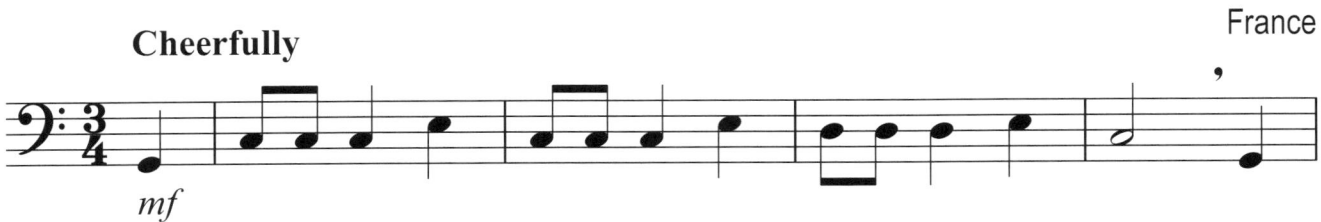

Izika Zumba
(Zulu war chant)

Fiercely — South Africa

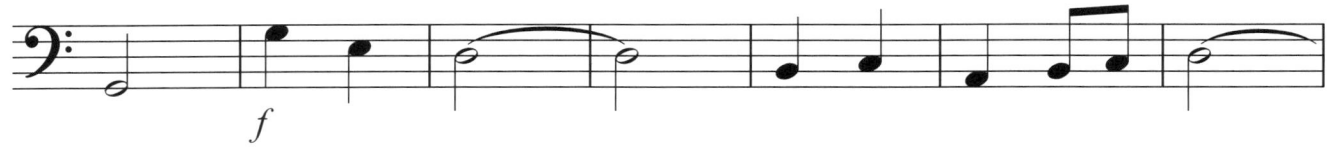

Can Can

Lively Jacques Offenbach

Botany Bay

Lively Australia

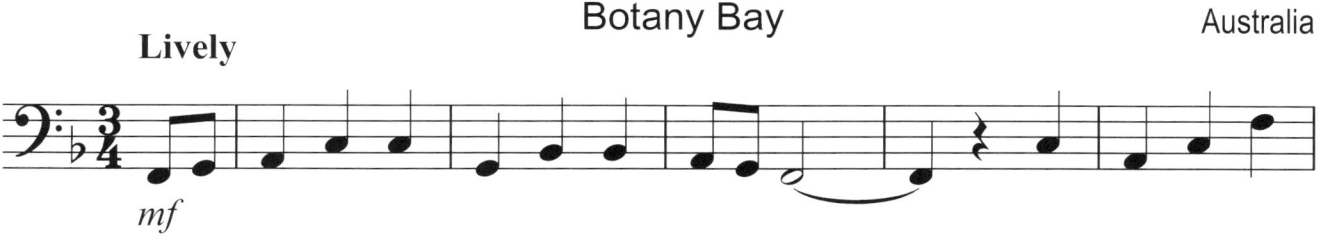

22

Tsetang Choung-La
Tibet

Jiana
Romania

Kisnay Baniya

Slowly — India

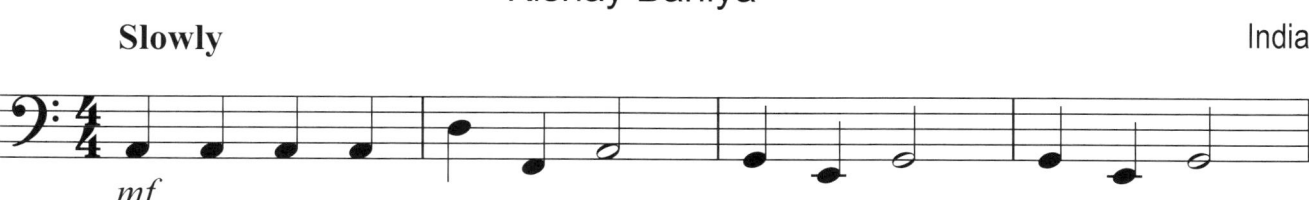

La Folia

Steadily — Spain

The Three Ravens

England

Cheerfully

Ah Ya Zein

Arabia

Smoothly

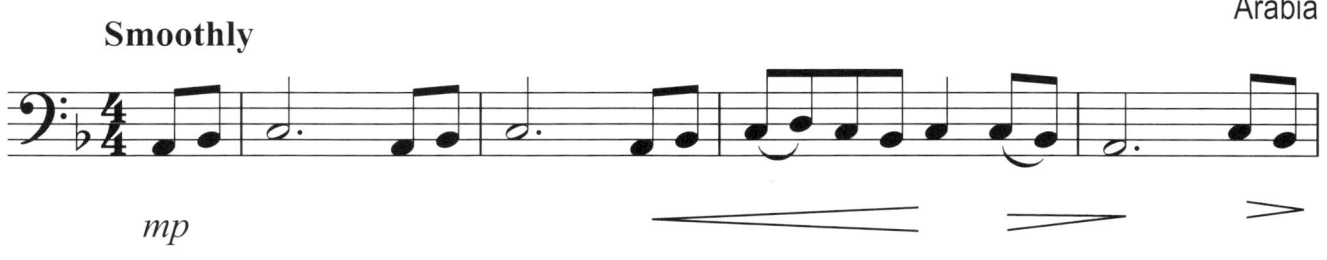

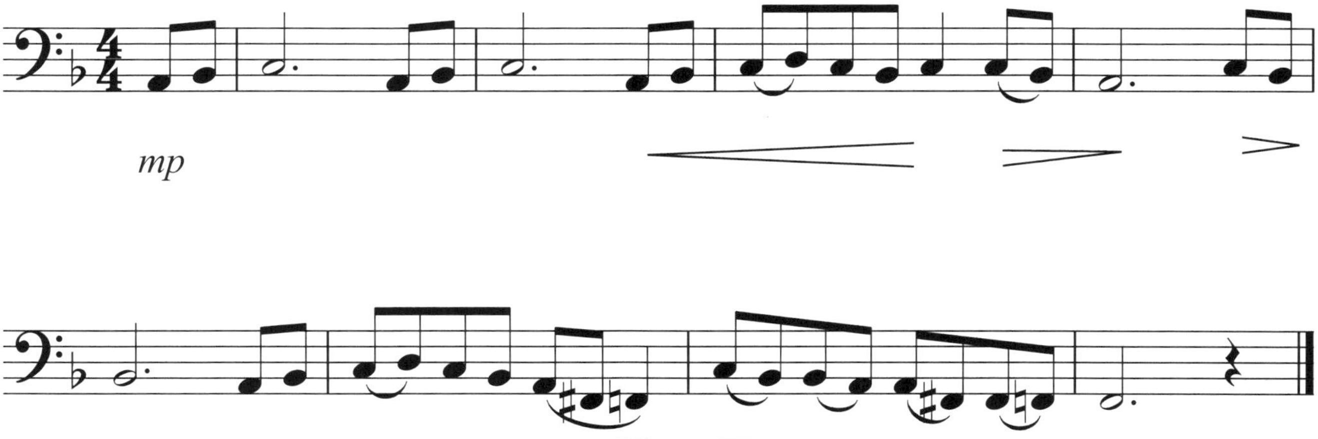

Come and Sing Together
(a round)

Hungary

Hey Ho, Nobody at Home
(a round)

England

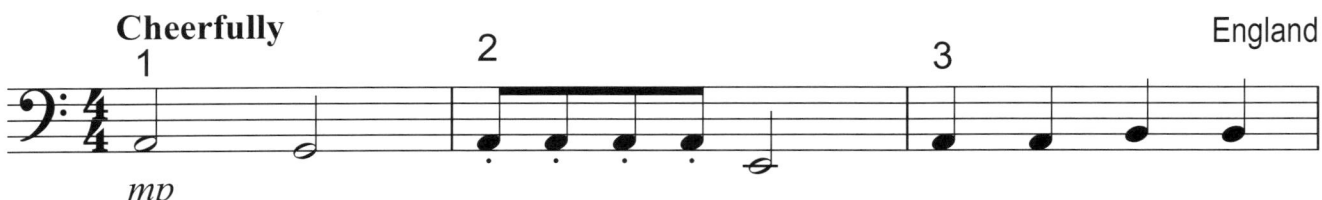
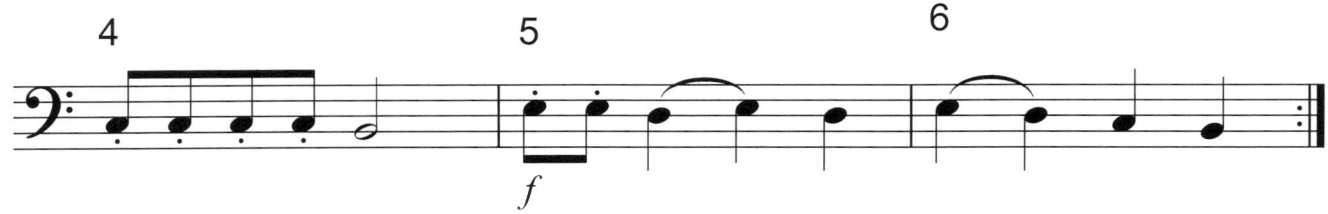

27

My Bird is Dead
(a round)

France

Mournfully

I Love Sixpence

England

Lovingly

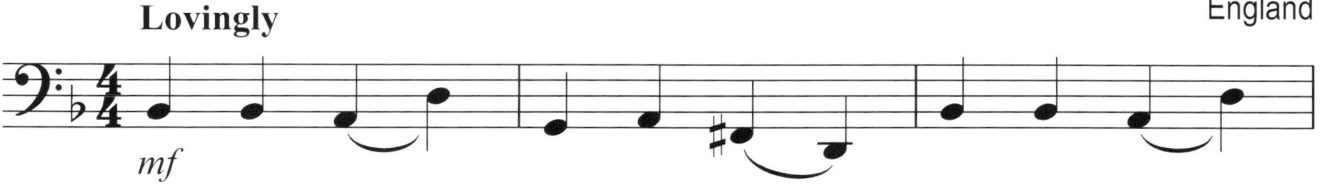

Early One Morning

England

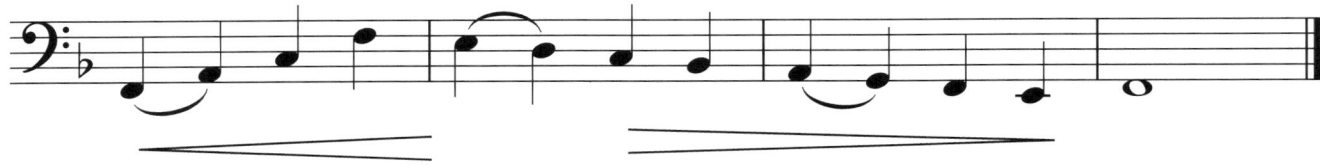

Rose, Rose
(a round)

England

Everybody Loves Saturday Night

Lively and fun Nigeria

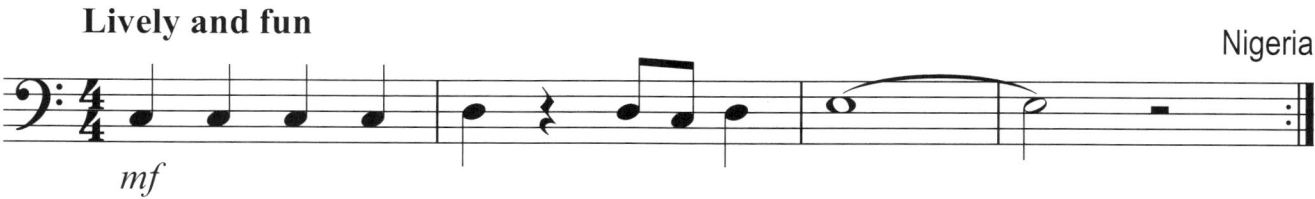
mf

Twinkle Twinkle Little Star

Smoothly France

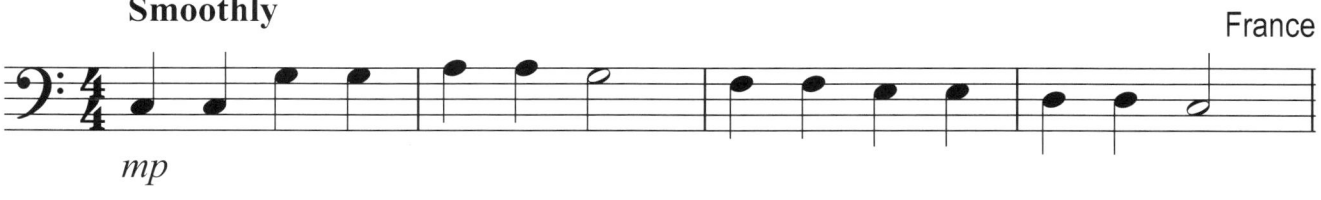
mp

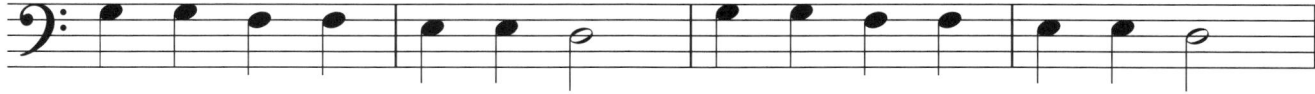

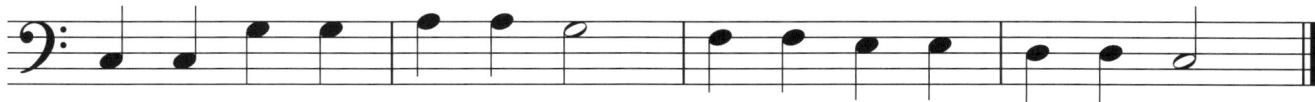

29

This Old Man

Cheerfully

England

mf

Johnny Todd

Not too fast

Scotland

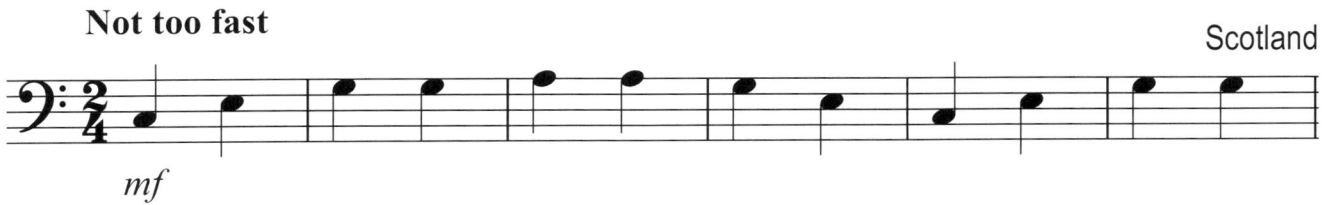

mf

Don't Forget Katie

Amanda Oosthuizen

Lively

mf

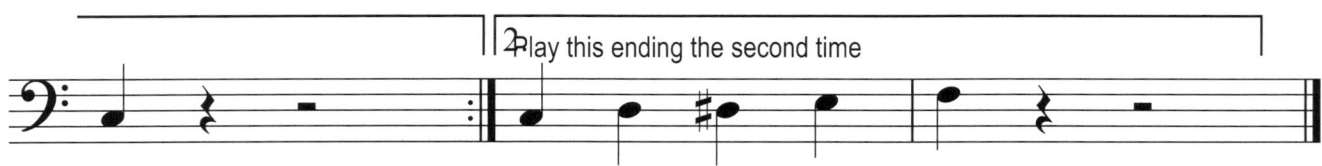

House of the Rising Sun

Mysteriously
USA

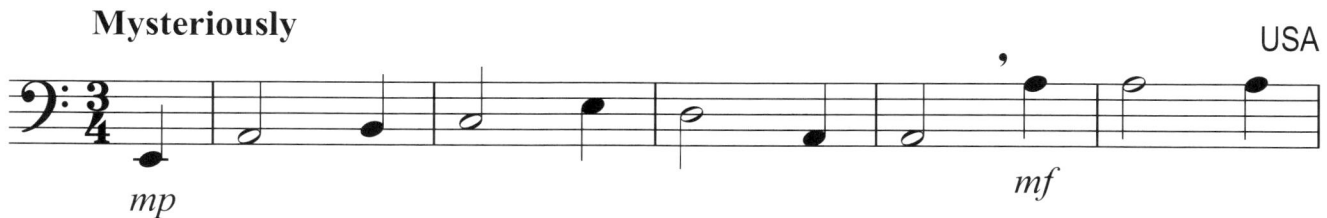

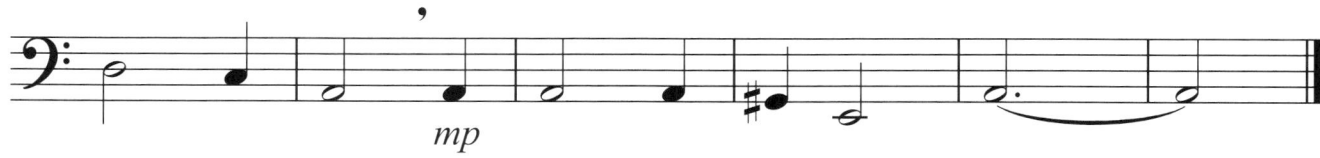

Shenandoah

Flowing
USA

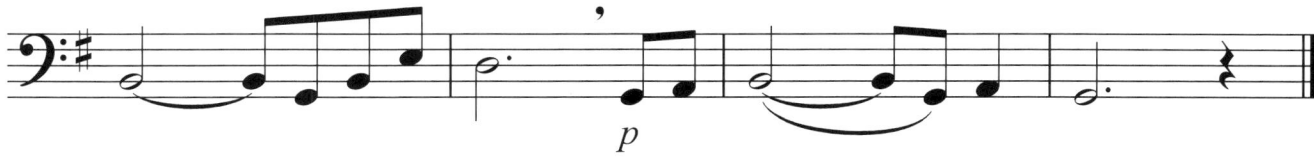

Cader Idris

Wales

Majestically

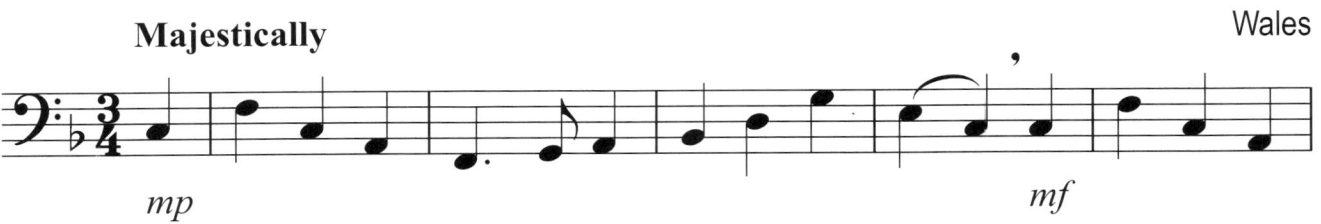
mp   *mf*

f

mf

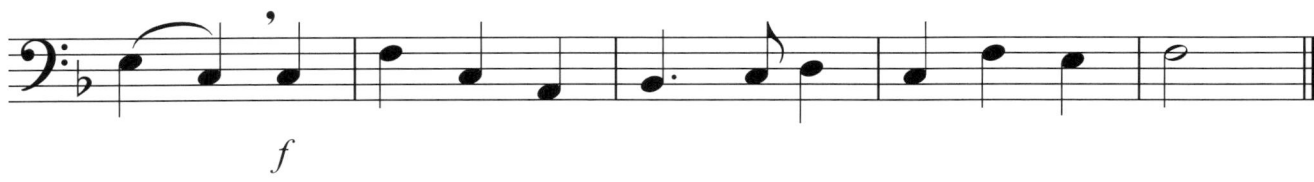
f

David of the White Rock

Wales

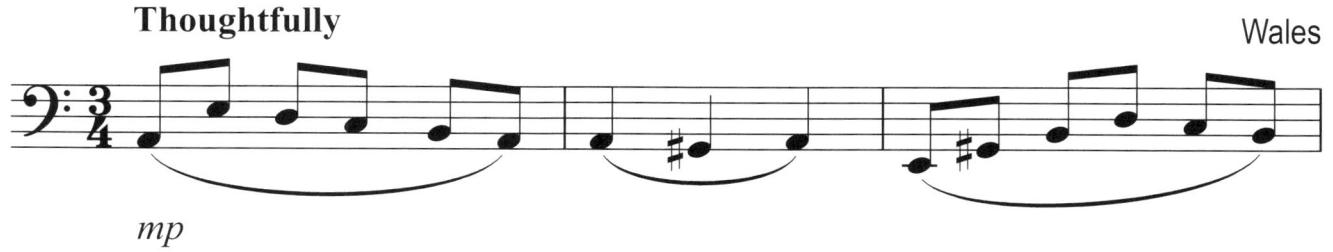

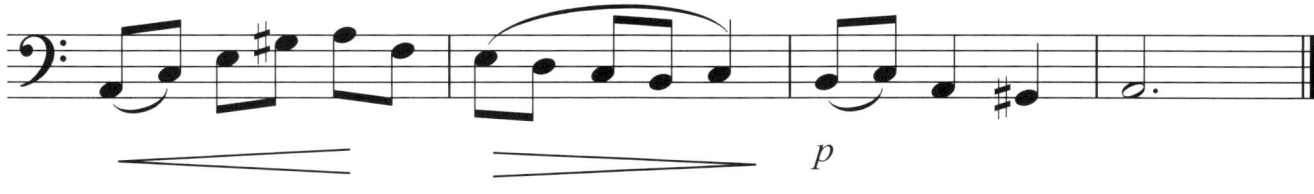

Greensleeves

England

Miss Lucy Long

USA

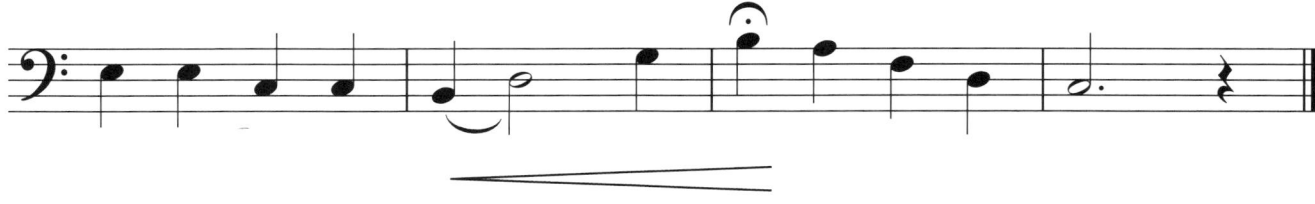

The Londonderry Air

Ireland

Smoothly

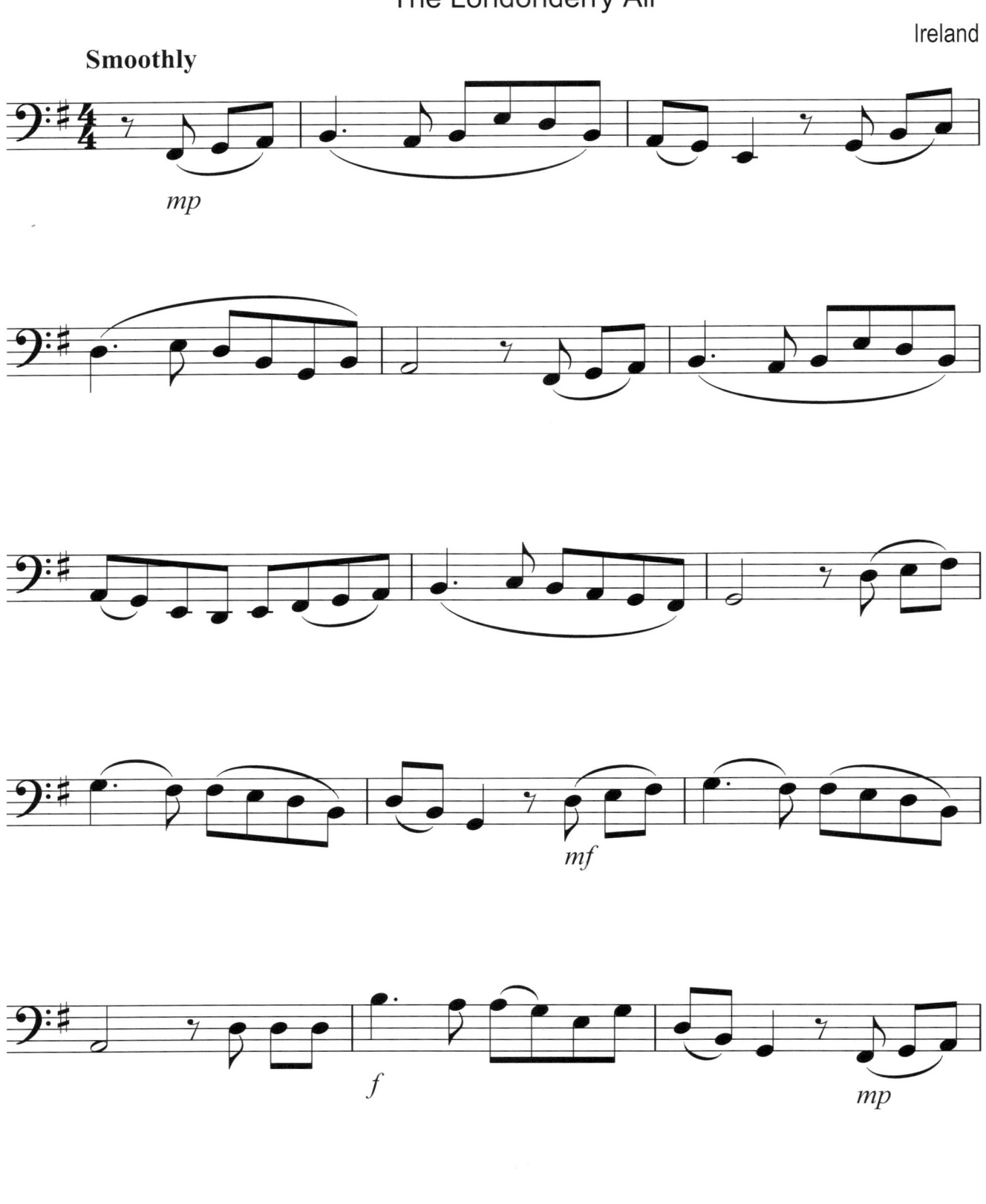

If you have enjoyed *Easy Tunes from Around the World,* why not try the other books in the series: Introducing:

50 Greatest Classics for Bassoon

The Brilliant Bassoon Book of Christmas Carols **Little Gems for Flute** **Dazzling Diamonds for Flute**

And for starting to play the flute or improving even more, try:
The Flying Flute Tune Book and Catch the Beat

The Flying Flute Tune Book has more than a hundred easy tunes. Based on note groups, easy to read, easy to play with tips on technique, music reading and improvisation from just three notes.

Catch the Beat is a sight reading practice book for flute with exercises to clap, jump, sing and tap, over 70 tunes to play, games activities and an easy way to score, making the challenges of sight reading fun and energetic for young players

Look out for more exciting music
Coming Soon

The Brilliant Bassoon Book of National Anthems
The Brilliant Bassoon Practice Book
The Brilliant Bassoon Book of Waltzes

Printed in Great Britain
by Amazon.co.uk, Ltd.,
Marston Gate.